For Quinn Thomson with love from Auntie Jeannie xx – J.W.

For my dad, Randle – R.C.

First published 2022 by Macmillan Children's Books
an imprint of Pan Macmillan
The Smithson, 6 Briset Street, London EC1M 5NR
EU representative: Macmillan Publishers Ireland Limited, 1st Floor,
The Liffey Trust Centre, 117–126 Sheriff Street Upper Dublin 1, D01 YC43
Associated companies throughout the world.
www.panmacmillan.com

ISBN (PB): 978-1-5290-4312-9

Text copyright © Jeanne Willis 2022
Illustrations copyright © Ross Collins 2022

Based on the original story *Through the Looking-glass and What Alice Found There*,
written by Lewis Carroll and illustrated by Sir John Tenniel,
first published by Macmillan & Co. Ltd in 1871

1 3 5 7 9 8 6 4 2

A CIP catalogue record for this book is available from the British Library.

Printed in China.

Alice Through the Looking-Glass

Jeanne Willis & Ross Collins

MACMILLAN CHILDREN'S BOOKS

Alice hugged her kitten as the
snowflakes kissed the pane.

"**Wicked puss!**" she said.
"**You stole my knitting wool again.
Behave yourself at once and
run along and chase a mouse,
or I'll send you through the mirror
into Looking-Glass House.**"

She climbed onto the mantelpiece –
the mirror turned to mist
and Alice disappeared
as if the glass did not exist.

She landed in another room and after some reflection, declared, **"It's just like home but in the *opposite* direction."**

She went into the garden
and spent the strangest hour
talking to some roses,
who mistook her for a flower.

"She's coming!" cried the daisies.
"Whoever do you mean?"
asked Alice and a Rose replied,
"The Queen! It's the Queen!"

"You must call me
'Your Majesty' and curtsey
if you will!"

The Red Queen said to Alice as they slowly climbed a hill.
"The world's a giant chess board! I wish that I could play,"
said Alice, "I would love to be a queen just for the day."
"You shall!" replied the Red Queen,"When you reach the final square
and the faster that we run along, the slower you'll be there."

The queen left Alice in a wood,
and underneath a tree,
she found two little men
called Tweedledum and Tweedledee.

"**Come,**" said Tweedledum,
"**It is time to start the battle.
Tweedledee has gone and
spoilt my nice, new rattle!**"

In their armour made from tea trays
and copper pots and pans,
the Tweedles blundered onwards
with their fearsome battle plans.

Suddenly the sky grew dark;
the brothers screamed, **"Oh no!"**
And they took to their heels, crying,
"It's the monstrous crow!"

Alice tried to hide among the trees, but she was seen!
Racing straight towards her was the messy old White Queen.

Alice pinned her shawl up
and dressed her long white hair.
How strange! Her brush and comb
were somehow tangled up in there!

A wild wind snatched the shawl away.
Alice shouted, **"Stop!"**
Running swiftly after it,
she found a little shop.

To her surprise the queen
had now become a woolly sheep.
Alice wondered if perhaps
she'd fallen fast asleep!

"I'd like to buy an egg,"
she said, pointing to the shelf.
"Fivepence farthing,"
baa'd the sheep.
"Fetch it down yourself!"

The chairs sprouted branches, the tables turned to trees.

The egg grew *enormous*, with a face and hands and knees.

"It's **Humpty Dumpty!**" Alice cried, "**Hold tight in case you fall.**"

"I've heard it happened once before ~ you tumbled off a wall."

"And so will all his men.

"The King will save me," Humpty said.

He's promised me they'll put me back together once again."

Alice sighed and tiptoed off
and prayed he wouldn't smash,
when suddenly, the forest shook
with one almighty

CRASH!

The White King and his soldiers
galloped through the wood,
then they all fell off their horses
as their riding wasn't good.

"What's happening?" asked Alice to a messenger called Hatta.

"Stuff and nonsense," he replied,

"It really doesn't matter.

The Lion and the Unicorn
are fighting for the crown.
Here come the drummers
to drum them out of town."

Covering her ears, Alice found another square.
"**Check!**" roared the Red Knight, falling off his mare,

"ALICE IS MY
PRISONER!"

"NO, SHE'S MINE, FIDDLE FADDLE!"

The White Knight declared
as he slipped from
his saddle.

The White Knight rode beside her,
then turned to say goodbye.
Alice reached the eighth square;
she was almost home and dry.
The grass was nice and soft
and feeling weary, she sat down . . .

"But what is this upon my head?"
It was a GOLDEN CROWN!

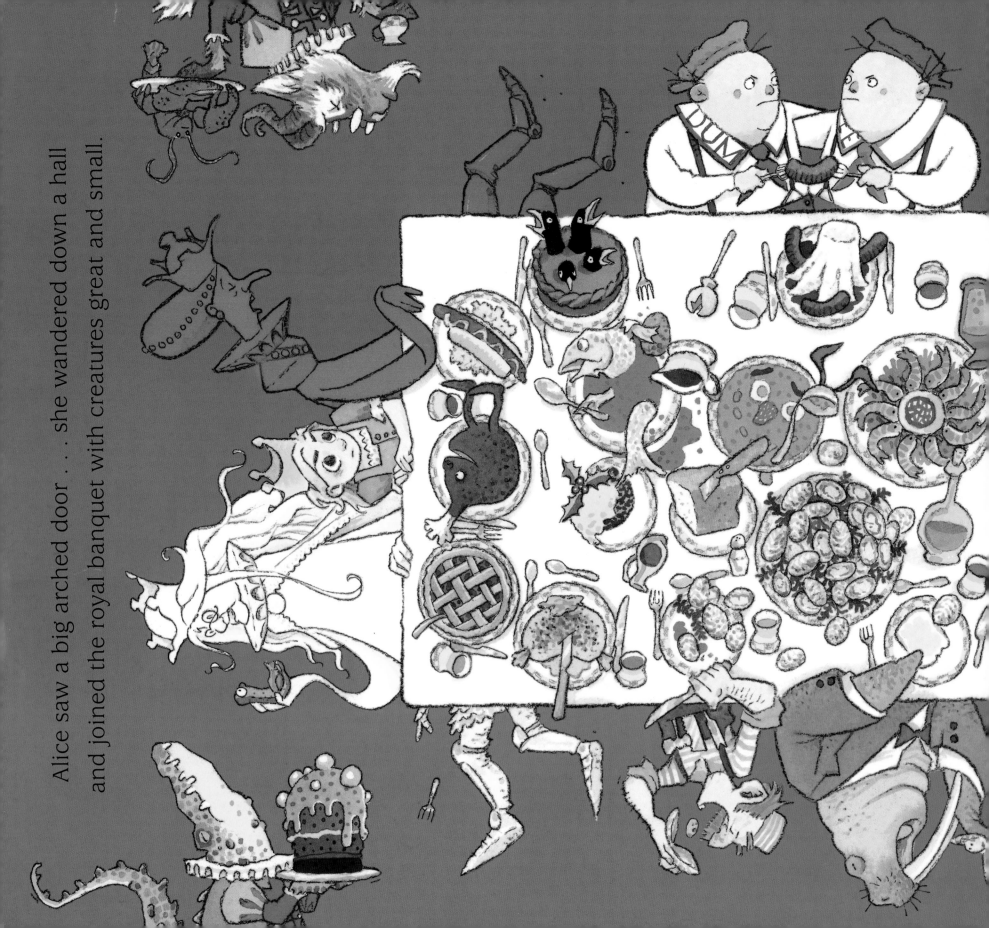

Alice saw a big arched door . . . she wandered down a hall and joined the royal banquet with creatures great and small.

The White Queen and the Red Queen were sitting next to her.

The Red Queen fell asleep and started snoring with a purr.

The mutton talked!
The pudding walked, to Alice's dismay,
and so . . . she grabbed the tablecloth
and whisked them all away.

She caught and shook the Red Queen,
who quickly shrank in size;
and turned into a furry kitten,
right before her eyes!

Alice found herself back home,
still sitting in her chair.
**"Did I go through the Looking-Glass?
Kitty, were you there?"**
She asked, **"Were you the Red Queen?
I'd really love to know . . ."**

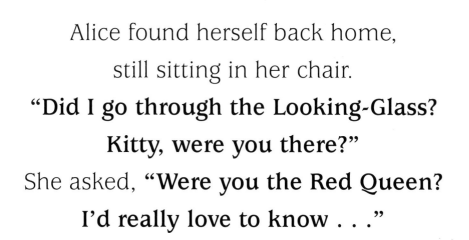

Perhaps you'll find the answer one day –
if you ever go!

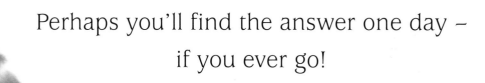

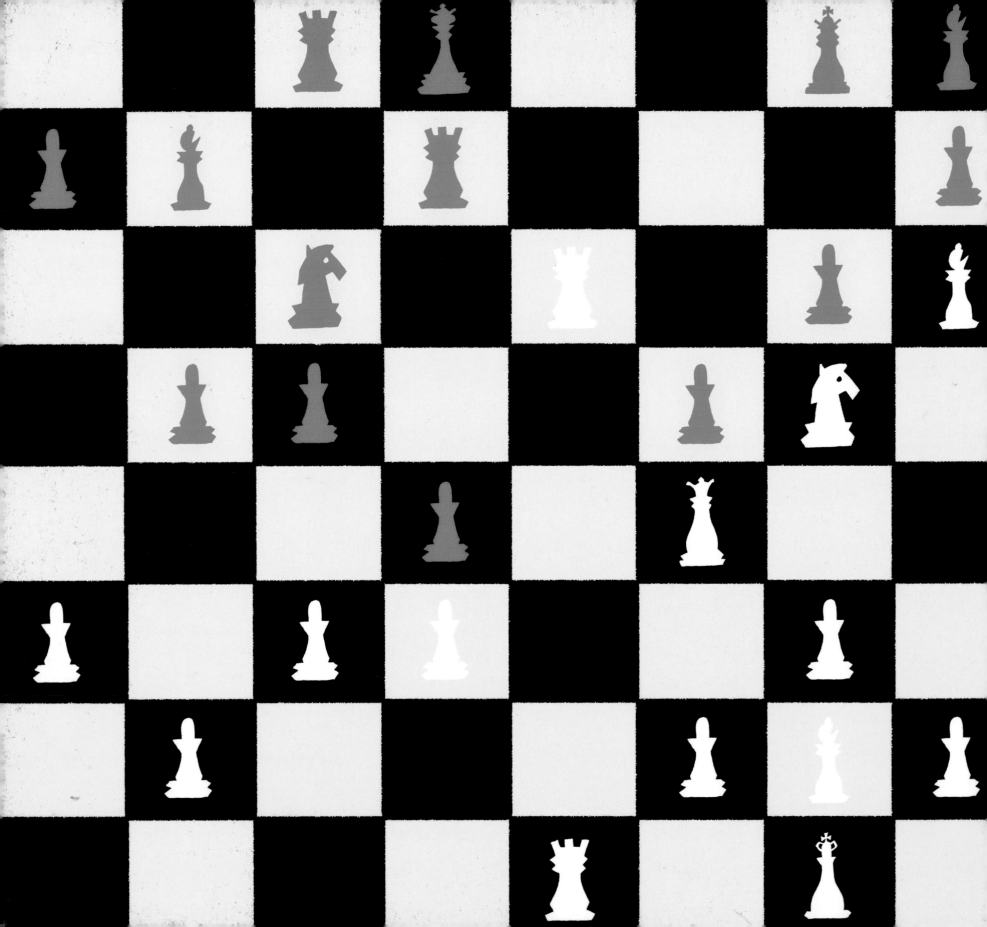